CW00853691

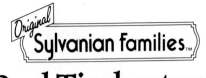

Bud Timbertop's
Sports Day

Simon Harwood

FANTAIL

BUD Timbertop is a very small brown bear who always seems to be in trouble. Not the naughty kind of trouble, more the accidental, 'that was a bit of bad luck' kind of trouble.

Chester Thistlethorn, the editor of the Sylvanian newspaper, once described Bud as an 'accident looking for somewhere to happen,' which was not very kind but really quite true.

ONE of the Sylvanians' favourite stories about Bud happened last Summer.

Bud was helping his father, Taylor Timbertop, paint the garden fence. After an hour, Bud took a step backwards to admire his work, and in doing so, stepped right into the tin of green paint that they were using!

Bud had a green foot for days and everyone joked about how he had taken an hour to paint six inches of fence but only taken two seconds to paint a whole bear's foot!

BUD didn't mind everyone joking and laughing about him as he's a cheerful sort of bear. In fact, he would say proudly:

"No one is ever miserable when I'm around."

But Bud had decided that it was time that he did something to make his mother, Rose Timbertop, proud of him.

"I know," Bud thought, "I'll win a gold medal at the School Sports Day."

BUD decided that in order to win a gold medal, he would have to get fit.

"What I need is lots of exercise and practice," he announced to a bemused Daisy. "Can I borrow your skipping rope for a couple of days?"

Daisy, Bud's young sister, just nodded her head and secretly wondered what disaster was about to descend upon her much loved brother.

BUD was in training!

"No more walking for me. I'll run everywhere and when I have to stay in one place, I'll do my running-on-the-spot or other exercises. I'll be so fit, I'll win everything," Bud said to nobody in particular as he ran down the garden path on his way to Rocky Babblebrook's General Store.

THE next day, Rose heard all about Bud's visit.

"He whirled in like a hurricane, stopped in front of the fruit stall and started running on the spot! Asked me which were better for athletes, apples or oranges? Chose an orange! Then off he went."

"He didn't break anything, did he?" questioned a resigned Rose.

With a note of wonder in his voice, Rocky had to admit that nothing was broken.

WHILE walking home, Rose met Aristotle Treefellow, the children's teacher.

"At school this morning..." started Aristotle.

"...Bud was running on the spot," finished Rose.

"And doing exercises, which included touching his toes!" continued Aristotle. "It was most upsetting, especially during prayers."

"I'll ask Taylor to have a few words with Bud this evening," Rose reassured Aristotle.

TAYLOR Timbertop is a big softy with his children and he is not keen on telling them off.

He eventually found Bud in the back garden. Bud was stepping up onto a box and then stepping down again. Taylor stood and watched him, and then asked: "Bud, what are you doing?"

Without stopping, Bud said:

"Building up my leg muscles."

"Oh," said Taylor, who was lost for words.

"I am going to win a gold medal for Mother," Bud offered as a further explanation.

"DID you tell Bud to stop terrorising Rocky and unnerving Aristotle?" Rose asked Taylor as he came in from the garden.

"Well, I didn't like to. You see, Bud wants to win a gold medal for you and I don't like to discourage my children," replied a sheepish Taylor.

"Taylor, you always leave it to me. Sometimes, I despair of you," said Rose, trying to sound cross and not to laugh at her husband's discomfort.

ROSE found Bud still stepping on and off the box.

"Bud, you must stop running-on-the-spot in Rocky's store and exercising during lessons."

"All right, Mother," replied a disheartened Bud.

"Bud, I would rather you didn't do anything in Rocky's store or in Aristotle's school room," said a wise Rose.

"Not even knee bends?" asked a dismayed Bud.

"No, not even knee bends," warned Rose.

"I'LL just have to exercise even harder when I can," decided Bud as he picked up the skipping rope for the last part of his nightly exercises before bedtime.

Taylor, who was watching from the window, suddenly realised what the exercises and gold medal had in common.

"Rose," Taylor called, "Bud must be getting ready for the School Sports Day next week."

"Of course," said Rose. "That means only one more week of worry."

THE next morning, bright and early, Bud was standing outside Rocky's store, exercising.

Rocky was getting out fresh vegetables so Crystal opened the shop.

"Good morning, Crystal," said Bud. "Have you got the entry forms for the School Sports Day yet?"

"Yes, I have," Crystal replied. "Would you like one?"

After thanking Crystal, Bud ran all the way home with his entry form safely tucked away in his back trouser pocket.

THE great day had arrived. By two o'clock all the parents had arrived to watch their children compete in the different events.

The first race was called and all the entrants lined up.

Smokey called: "Ready, steady, go!"

They were off, with Bud leading the way.

But, at the finish line, it was Logan Evergreen who came in first, closely followed by Rusty Wildwood.

THE second race was over hurdles. Barnaby won that. Lester won the sack race and Hollie won the discus.

"There are still a lot more events," said a cheerful Bud as he went to the long jump sand-pit.

But Bud didn't win that either.

"I am bound to do well in the egg and spoon race," he said hopefully.

"Bud, have you entered every race and event?" asked Rose.

"Yes, of course," replied Bud.

THE egg and spoon race was very hectic. In the end, it was a race between Bluebell Oakwood and Bud. But who would cross the finish line first?

With a last second mad rush, it was Bud! He was so excited that he flung his arms in the air.

But he had forgotten all about his egg! It landed right on top of his head!

Everyone laughed, even Bud.

"I'll win two gold medals for you next year," Bud told his mother.

FANTAIL PUBLISHING, AN IMPRINT OF PUFFIN ENTERPRISES

Published by the Penguin Group
27 Wrights Lane, London W8 5TZ, England
Viking Penguin Inc., 40 West 23rd Street, New York, NY 10010, USA
Penguin Books Australia Ltd, Ringwood, Victoria, Australia
Penguin Books Canada Ltd, 2801 John Street, Markham, Ontario, Canada L3R 1B4
Penguin Books (NZ) Ltd, 182-190 Wairau Road, Auckland 10, New Zealand
Penguin Books Ltd, Registered Offices: Harmondsworth, Middlesex, England

First published by Fantail Publishing, 1989
13579108642
Copyright © 1989 Epoch Co Ltd
All rights reserved

014 0900152

Made and printed in Great Britain by
William Clowes Limited
Beccles and London